One Night
in the Zoo

Picture books by Judith Kerr

First published in Great Britain by HarperCollins Publishers in 2009

10 9 8 7 6 5 4 3 2 1
ISBN: 978-0-00-732112-4

HarperCollins Children's Books is a division of HarperCollins Publishers Ltd.
Text and illustrations copyright © Kerr-Kneale Productions Ltd 2009
The author/illustrator asserts the moral right to be identified as the author/illustrator of the work.
A CIP catalogue record for this title is available from the British Library.

Visit our website at: www.harpercollins.co.uk

Printed and bound by Printing Express, Hong Kong

One Night in the Zoo

Judith Kerr

HarperCollins *Children's Books*

One magical, moonlit night in the zoo

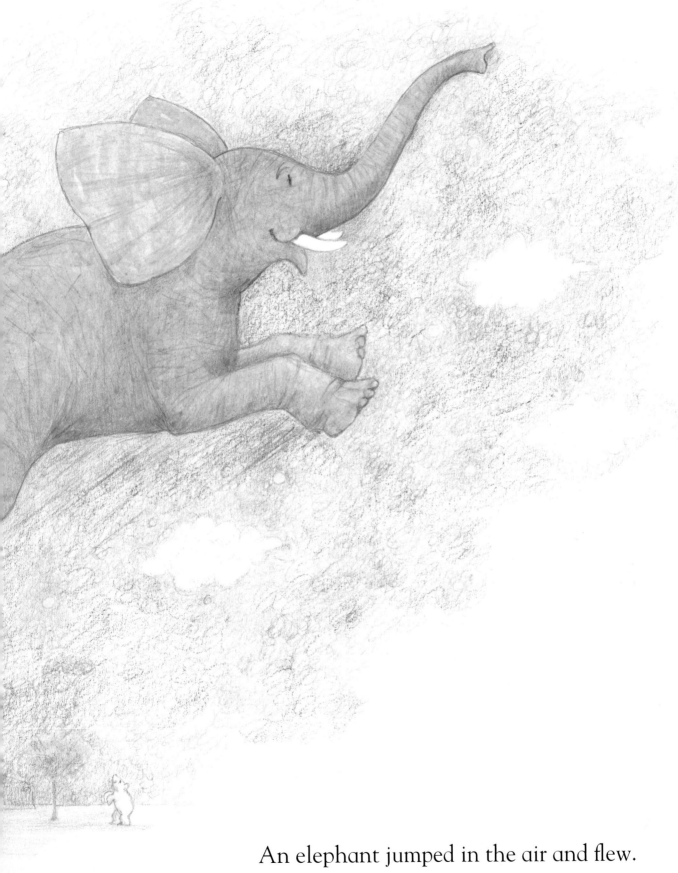

An elephant jumped in the air and flew.
But nobody knew.

Then a crocodile and a kangaroo
Set off on a bicycle made for two,

And three lions did tricks which astonished a gnu.
But nobody knew.

Four bears cooked a squid and squidgeberry stew

Which turned five flamingos
from pink to blue.

Six rabbits climbed a giraffe for the view.
But nobody knew.

Seven tigers sneezed: Atchoo! Atchoo!
Atchoo! Atchoo! Atchoo! Atchoo!
ATCHOO! And their seven sneezes blew
The feathers off a cockatoo.

Eight monkeys stuck them back with glue.
But nobody knew.

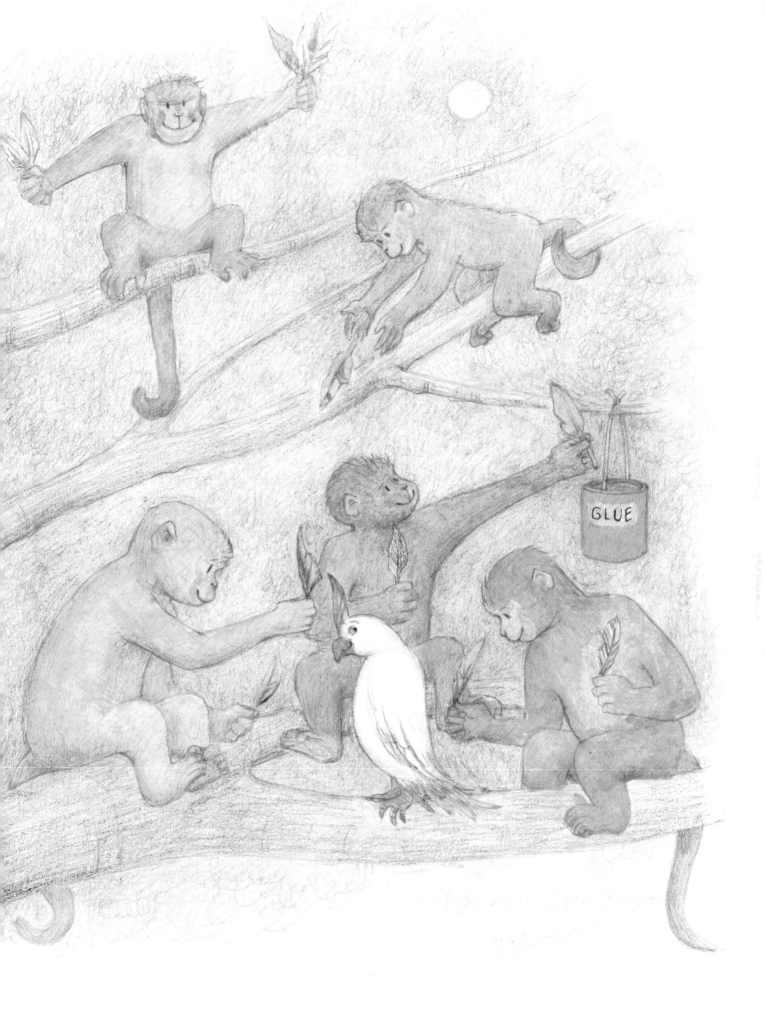

Then in the sky a pinkish hue
Broke through the dark, and as it grew
Nine owls cried, "Woo! Terwitterwoo!
The night is fading! Quickly! Shoo!
Back in your cages, all of you!"

The sun got up. The keeper, too.
Ten cocks crowed, "Cockadoodledoo!
He's coming! Quick! He's almost due!"

The keeper and his trusty crew
Found all the animals back on view
(excepting only just one or two).

"They look so tired," he said. "All through
That moonlit night what did they do?"
But nobody knew…

...except you!